MIRACLES COME ON MONDAYS

PENELOPE CRAY

MIRACLES COME ON MONDAYS

PLEIADES
P R E S S

The Robert C. Jones Short Prose Series
Warrensburg, Missouri

Library of Congress Control Number:
ISBN: 9780807173008

Published by Pleiades Press

School of English
University of Central Missouri
Warrensburg, Missouri 64093

Distributed by Louisiana State University Press

Cover Image: Bill McDowell, "Untitled (ice on grass)" 2016. Inkjet print. 16" x 20"
Author photo by Catherine Karapuda
Book design by Steve Budington
Interior design by David Wojciechowski

First Pleiades Printing, 2020

Financial support for this project has been provided by the University of Central Missouri, and the Missouri Arts Council, a state agency.

To Steve, Finn, and Vita

TABLE OF CONTENTS

III

MOUNTAIN

A woman cannot speak but by comparison. *What I am feeling is not what she is feeling. What she has is not mine.* The woman has a first daughter who is not the same as her second daughter, who is not the same as the mother or the second daughter of a second mother to whom the mother compares herself and her second daughter. *That mother is not unlike my own mother*, the woman decides, pleased to have identified a place akin to kinship, but safer, it seems to her. There, she might parade the battered sheep of her childhood before the dull curs of her adult years, whom she labors to keep sated. *But,* she continues, *I am so unlike my mother, so undesirous of what she desired, that I must be nothing like that other mother either, who is somewhat like my mother and also somewhat unlike her, and perhaps entirely. She is less beautiful, though her daughters, beautiful and successful, are nothing like my own.* She imagines her daughters, thick-armed and wild-haired, chipping away at their occupations as indentured laborers might chip away at the foot of a mountain. Her daughters have inherited every possible inch of impossibility from her and her mother before her, and the mountain has been there a long time—has been there, it seems now to the mother, before the incomprehensible burst of the universe first divided this from that.

THIS AND THAT

This is what I wanted and I got what I wanted.

That's what I wanted: to ask for what I wanted and to get what I wanted. Two things.

What I wanted was to ask for what I wanted, which is this, which I got.

The first of the two things—to ask for what I wanted—is not secondary to the second of the two things—to get what I wanted—but equal in importance.

But is the wanting the same as the asking?

What I wanted more than asking for what I wanted was to want what I wanted.

Wanting, in the form of asking, and wanting what I got, which was this.

That is what I wanted. This was that.

DEATH DEVOURS MORE THAN NADINE

Each week, one of Nadine's doctor friends appeared at her four-poster bed and amputated another piece of Nadine. Her artist friends wept with their sketchpads in the doorway and returned with portraits of the missing parts. Nadine was to select from these—some of them simple line drawings, others trompe l'oeil masterpieces—the portrait that had achieved the greatest likeness. It was not, of course, the accuracy that mattered but how the portrait invoked the spirit of the missing. Who better to recognize the true essence of Nadine's severed hand than Nadine?

Weeks passed. Nadine shrank. The portraits—of Nadine's thumbs, index fingers, then Nadine's three-fingered hands, her handless wrists, her elbows, her feet, her footless calves, her knees and thighs, her buttocks—lined the walls of her bedroom, propped against the baseboard until Nadine had announced their optimal exhibition. The artists schooled the doctors as to where and how to make the cut, eager for each portion to embody Nadine's rare beauty.

When the time came for Nadine's mouth to go, her entourage lost hope. How now—handless, footless, *mouthless*—would she communicate which of her portraits was the best? Nadine's blue eyes watched the doorway for the portraits of her mouth, but none appeared. In the end, only one of the doctors, who secretly wished to be an artist, took a stab at it. That he should win by default was only fair. Nadine's eyes scanned the room, her hundreds of portraits stacked in silence. She saw the moon rise and, later, the sun.

In the morning, the doctors carried away her eyes, no need now to cut. The artists rallied for the last portrait, which, they'd agreed, the doctors would judge. The artists took turns laying their portraits of Nadine's eyes on her pillow, just as they had been—azure, cerulean, opaline—inclined toward the window where now one could see a red bird in the maple. The doctors, having no firm criteria for judging excellence, refused to choose a winner, and the artists fell into argument. Unobserved in their portraits, Nadine's eyes grew wide a final time and then fell into rapture.

THE JAR

I keep my father in a jar, his hands smaller than my fingernail, his fingers now like the fingers of a newt. The jar is heaven for my father, his what-came-after perfectly preserved in formaldehyde. The jar has a miniature whirlpool feature that moves my father when I want him to, twirls my father like a ballerina and otherwise lets him loose to drift to the bottom, an autumn leaf. If I set the jar before a red wall, my father lives in a red world and is brutal and pulls at his mouth; against green, serene, his hands silent for hours. Who is my father? His fingers grope against the glass, crimp in complicated gestures, pressed between his heart and the jar, their tiny pads yellow with pressure or laced into his thatch of ebony hair. In certain lights it seems he is hardly there, tucked into the jar's fat glass base, hidden for an instant by some trick of, surely, the eye.

GOD OF MODERATION

God loves the medium trees, the middling grasses, the tepid breeze. Not the short, not the tall. The mid-size sedan. The average afternoon. The family at the shore under cloud cover. The moderate apology. The fear that passes quickly. The fleeting thought that returns and flees and returns. The mediocre bath, the lukewarm review, the day-old bagel, the poet with a day job, the every-other-weekend warrior, the mild cheddar. These God praises and blesses and makes plentiful. All else, he condemns to Heaven or Hell.

DISAPPEARANCE

They would be monsters with everyone but each other. He donned his ogre outfit in his car before work. After he left, she put on her harpy haberdashery. To each other, they were tender, beautiful only. But then he was invited to work parties and her coworkers insisted she join them for happy hour. They would go once, maybe twice a week, they agreed. On those days, they were in costume from dawn to well after dusk and, once home, they were too exhausted to undress. No matter. They each knew the other. They could see through the disguises. She hadn't meant to flinch when she encountered him in the dark on her way to the bathroom. He hadn't meant to grimace when she sat across from him over a late dinner, her costume rumpled, a little too lived-in for his liking. Without their old breaks from the pretense, they began to see the other only as they appeared, began to believe, too, that they were who they met in the mirror.

THE SHAPE OF A BIRD'S MISFORTUNE

Today there is one bird pecking at my spleen. Yesterday there were two birds and the day before three. I hide my spleen under my favorite shirt, but still the bird gets in there. Yet, one bird is good, better than two and much better than three. I think, if my spleen had teeth, the bird could be ingested as a sort of nourishment. Instead the bird irritates; my spleen is sore and complains. I can think of nothing else, and therefore nothing that is not the bird. But just one bird today, where yesterday there were two and the day before three. What is the shape of progress inside a sub-par environment, when escape is not possible and life must be measured as the relative extremity of multiple misfortunes? Is it the shape of a bird? And what is the shape of a bird's misfortune? Is it the shape of a spleen its friends have abandoned that cries out still to be pecked?

THE PAST MUST BE INVENTED

One way forward is to forget to remember. Another is to remember to forget. The forgetting is for the purpose not of remembering later but of not remembering ever, which is to say for the purpose of leaving the dismembered self scattered across the past, as sand, as dust. The past may be a lap with two large knees squeezed together at the end of two broad thighs so that nothing falls through, not sand, not dust. It may be that these two large knees rise up and the contents of the lap slide together, aligned in the ravine between the two broad thighs. In this way, meaning may be made, but casually, unintentionally, as sand, as dust. The meaning may be logical, but because it was meaning thrown together and not manufactured through dogged endeavor, the meaning is nothing, not sand, not dust.

INTROVERT

Add water indefinitely to a small pile of salt. There will be those whose thirst is quenched.

After the prescribed amount of added water, they will no longer taste the salt.

The salt will become to them useful differently, in a way not given to salt.

That the salt was there at all—that once it was *all* that was there—will be lost on those whose thirst is quenched.

What is wanted is to remove the water. What is wanted is never to have added the water in the first place.

The water is over here, conforming to the shape of its container.

This water has no salt. The salt is over there, in its own pile.

Water contains no salt and salt contains no water. Do not say, that pile of salt is so small we could add water to it and still quench our thirst.

There is the knowing the salt is there.

That is the knowing one wishes not to dilute.

MIRACLES COME ON MONDAYS

She'd been explaining as she made the lunch he would eat later at the office that she believed in God because it made her feel better, not because she was convinced of God's existence. He had found this unreasonable, but anyway, he was late for work. There was no time to return to reason.

After he was gone, she decided she would vacuum the couch. Mr. Cat had spent the winter curled on the throws draped over the vintage velvet, and while she would sometimes launder the top one or two throws, she could not think of the last time she'd stripped the couch bare. Before they got Mr. Cat and for some time after, they'd left the couch exposed, its claret velvet calling to them to sit, drink wine, feed each other strawberries.

She'd noticed the first tear not long after Mr. Cat celebrated his second birthday.

"That's sixteen in human years, you know. He's a teenager now," she'd said.

"Yes," he'd agreed. It was a tear.

They'd patched it with a miracle product he recalled from an infomercial, and she'd brought home the first throw soon after. Then Lucy arrived, nine months after their only cruise vacation—an all-inclusive package, a bona fide good deal—and the couch gradually lost its shape to layers of fleece and chenille.

One day they would uncover it. When Mr. Cat was dead and Lucy off to college, they'd lie naked together on its sensuous curves, murmuring instead of shouting across rooms or from the top of stairs, their heads no longer cocked to one side, the better to listen for what and how the other had heard.

The couch's bulk seemed almost to breathe. She had parented herself through several self-help regimens and owned two tarot decks, wrapped still in their silk. She had parted ways with masturbation, if for no other reason than it no longer asked for her by name as it once had, an all-time favorite song that now sounded tinny. Her days seemed now like rocks at the bottom of a wishing well, coarse lumps among the shining coins.

Their early lovemaking had been exquisite, the passion between them an endless loop. It was that passion that caused them to see, truly see, the couch when, deep in the anteroom of an antique shop in Newport, Rhode Island, he had leaned over her, his breath passing from his open mouth into her nostrils. She'd lost her balance and slipped backward onto the velvet sheen of this piece of major furniture. It had been unexpectedly cool against the palms of her hands, pressed flat in instinct to catch her weight. Despite its impracticality, their mutual giddiness overcame their reservations. At the end of their vacation, he had driven it back to their apartment in a U-Haul while she followed behind in their Civic. She imagined what they would do on their new purchase, silent in the darkness behind the truck's metal roller-door.

Mr. Cat meowed at her from the couch, stretching, offering to be stroked.

"Off you go," she said, dropping him onto his paws. She surveyed the mass of blankets. They'd need to be washed. All of them. There was no point in vacuuming throw rugs.

She removed the blankets, each one overlapping part of another. What evidence was there here of unreason? Did he ever have to ask her to calm down when they fought?

She encountered the nest under the fifth blanket. The mice had chewed a small hole in the velvet and dragged the scraps into the soft triangle of darkness formed between two cushions and the back of the couch. It was not the nest that caught her attention first but the holes and what they could signify. No cigarettes in the house. No moths that she had noticed. She peered in and, there, the mass of hairless bodies undulating, wriggling to get down under each other away from the light. Filth. That's what he would call them. That would be his word. But she marveled, at their brazen reproduction and birthing of how many generations season after season, and all of it unfolding beneath their thighs and buttocks, her toes tucked up under her, as they watched the screen. That was oblivion. Filth. That repulsive not knowing.

The impulse came not as a thought so much as a tingling sensation in her taste buds that built almost to an ache. She reached into the dark triangle and lifted the infant on top into the light. Its pink limbs groped the air.

"Shhh," she whispered to its blind features, her lips brushing the downy nostrils no bigger than a freckle. Then she opened her mouth and let the pink animal wriggle on her tongue.

DON'T BE RUDE

First the itch says "leg," but I don't believe it. I itch my arm. "Leg," says the itch.

I hitch my skirt and pull the back of my knee into view. A red dot, a bubble freckle, hidden by the too-tall lip of my knee sock. I sit down to look. The back of my knee has grown a small itchy friend.

My brother bugs me when he's had it with being dead. He tells me not to tell Momma and when I think of telling her, he makes my leg itch. Now I get it. I scratch him hard to be done with him. He was not my fault. Me and the girls knew he'd be going. He never loved any of his toys—not like I love the girls. He left his fire truck in the rain and it grew mold on its plastic yellow belly.

He was only a little brother. I could hold his foot in the palm of my hand and pretend he was dancing there. He didn't know how to bring his toys in from the rain. He didn't know how to put on his rain jacket. He fell right off the fire truck. The girls told me about the freckle on the back of my knee, that they'd seen him hiding there. I guess being dead made him even smaller. I don't know how to keep track of him now. I might lose him down the bathtub drain. But when I try to rub him off, I can't, and I feel better.

His room always smelled like diapers. I never smelled like that. The girls told me it was a good idea to let some air in. Momma says the cold air didn't do it, but I'm not so sure. I left the window open when she wasn't looking and let the death come in. He was so little, he needed only a little bit of death to do the job.

Then Momma has to change the new baby's diaper. I tell her he's too small and she keeps crying. "Happy tears," she sings. I touch the skin on the back of my knee and he's still there. I feel the nub of him.

Momma's always asking us to believe things that aren't true. She says she can't believe them by herself. Believing takes research. You have to find out who else believes it and who doesn't. If we believe with her, her research will be easier. She wants things to be easier. I tell her I will eat my peas but my not carrots and she cries again.

The baby sleeps all day and all night. Momma changes his diaper and he sleeps some more. The back of my knee itches and keeps me awake. His poops stink because Momma can't change a diaper that small. Then I have a funny idea and get a knife from the kitchen. The girls tell me it won't hurt, but it does and my screaming wakes Momma. I don't tell her she wiped up my baby brother when she wiped up the blood.

The girls tell me I need a plan for letting Momma know where the baby is. I point at the trash, but Momma says I don't need that blood anymore. She says it wasn't mine, it was hers, the part of her that bled right out of me. I didn't know Momma was going to leave like that with the baby. I hear him crying in there, but it doesn't bother her. She doesn't go into the trash with him. She tells me to go to sleep, and I hear my bedroom door click when she leaves. And I hear the crying. I hear everything.

It's light out when the door opens again. I'm awake, pretending that me and the girls are on a cruise. Taste the salty air, they tell me. Momma's watching, and I stick out my tongue.

FRECKLE

He has a freckle on the inside of his middle toe.

Look, he says to me one night in our bed, prying his toes apart.

There's a small brown dot where the sinewy inside of his long toe meets the round flesh of his foot pad.

What does it mean? he asks.

It's a door, I say. *It leads to the many fine passageways of your body.*

What's in there? he wants to know.

All the joys of your life, I say, *with their days and times marked.*

He looks dubious. I imagine him counting the joys and finding them too few.

I don't think I want to know that, he says. *I prefer to be surprised.*

That's why no one can enter their own freckle, I say, as one interpretation of a true story.

SPIRAL

When I was a child, all baths ended with a spiral. I watched the bathwater drain and saw myself inside the spiral, sometimes on the inner rings, sometimes the outer. As an adult, I saw my life that way. I was on the inside or the outside, but I was always part of the spiral.

Now, when I take a bath, there's no spiral when the water drains. The spiral costs extra. In place of the inner and outer rings, there is only a gradual going down, the sucking sound of the drain, the level of water, cloudy with soap and dirt, sinking lower.

How did they manage to take something so basic from me? How did I let them?

AIR GUITAR

Annette opened the case and a guitar-shaped vapor wafted up and hovered above her lap.

Her father swelled. "It's an air guitar," he said.

The kettle whistled in the kitchen.

"You sit, Bill, I'll get it," her mother said breezily, rising from the couch.

"Don't get too close this time, Gladys," her father called.

Annette's mother deflated a little at her husband's remark and bumped her crown on the door as she floated into the kitchen.

"She's always been so clumsy," Annette's father huffed. "Thank goodness you haven't inherited *that* from her."

Annette strummed the air guitar.

"That's it, you'll have the hang of it in no time," her father said. His eyes narrowed. "Looking around to see if that's all, eh?"

Annette nodded out of habit. The pressure had been getting to her lately. If she didn't inflate soon, her father would never forgive her. He handed her another box. Annette pulled off the lid. It contained a small pool of water.

"It's a mood cloud," said her father. "When you're sad, it will rain on your head, and when you're happy, it will turn white and fluffy and move to the side to let the sun shine down. Now we won't always have to be guessing what you're feeling."

The cloud condensed above Annette's head, where it released a cold drizzle.

"I wonder why it's doing that," said her father, reaching for the manual.

Annette shivered and glanced at her father's air pressure dial. The arm wavered, then began to climb. The whistling sound in the kitchen trailed off. Then BLAM!

"Oh, Christ, not again," he hissed.

Annette trailed after her father into the kitchen, where her mother had exploded.

"Gladys! That's the third balloon you've burst this month! Do you think we're made of money?"

"Sorry, dear," Annette's mother's voice sang from the ceiling. "I forget this latex makes me so reactive."

"I had to marry an oxygen tank," Annette's father puffed.

"I wasn't a tank when you met me; I was a canister."

"Is that what you call it? My mother warned me that giddy routine would get on my nerves. Why couldn't I settle down with a nice mattress pump like my father."

"Oh, that old bag's as full of hot air as any of us. Just gather me up, will you?"

"Annette, get the hot water bottle from the bathroom," her father wheezed.

Annette shot an uneasy look in her mother's direction. She could almost discern the shape of her panic. The mood cloud's drizzle lightened to a fine mist. It was pleasant, refreshing even.

"No!" Gladys was saying, "I don't want to go in the water bottle—"

"Hush, it's the perfect place for you. Annette?"

"But it's dark in there. I'll go in the light bulb."

"You haven't fit in the light bulb since you had Annette!"

"I won't go in the bottle! Annette, please, get the pickle jar. Annette? Bill, what's wrong with Annette?"

Bill turned to his daughter in the doorway. She was strumming a tune on the air guitar. The cloud above her had turned white and fluffy and moved to the side. The sun blazed onto her hands as they worked the air strings. Tiny sparks shot from her fingers.

"Annette? Sweetheart?"

Annette's smile flickered through the leaping flames. She was growing distant, epically remote. The vacuum Annette left behind roared ever louder as it devoured her father.

"Oh, my Bill! Oh, my Annette!" Gladys giggled from the ceiling.

PILLAR

Grace lay on the couch, fidgeting. The man had promised he wouldn't shrink her and asked only her name.

Grace.

Grace?

Yes.

I won't shrink you, Grace.

I want to stay my size.

What is your size, Grace?

You won't shrink me?

I won't shrink you.

My jeans, my shoes, my bed.

What is your size about your bed? Did you make it yourself?

This morning I did.

Of course.

My underwear, my belt, my toothbrush.

Your teeth?

Yes, they are my size, too.

Not shrunken.

No.

Neither too large.

That's right.

What if I said I wanted to brutalize you into language?

With your hands?

With my mind.

With your imaginary hands?

With my mind.

With your imaginary mind?

Sure.

I'd say, No, thank you.

I see.

And I'd remind you that you promised not to shrink me.

Grace, you are not insane. I will give you a note to take home to your mother.

Thank you. Shall I pay you in salt or pepper?

Salt, that I may turn to it in times of need, which surely await me.

CHOSEN ONE

I choose this corner of the room. No one makes me choose. I choose; it's my choice.

The others are choosing too, though their parts of the room don't seem like choosing. To stand just off-center from the center of the room, or near a doorway where people who have yet to choose are entering, is conveniently nonspecific choosing.

If here, why not there?

I crouch. That's choosing too. Most stand—another choice that goes unremarked—or lean, choosing wall space. Ironic.

Not like crouching. Not like choosing the corner—in my case, the result of two sloping walls that form a low wedge of ceiling above my crouch. The crouch then is a response to the corner, to its ceiling. It has meaning because it is contextual. Responsive. I respond to my corner, which is to say I respond to my choosing.

Yet most would say, why choose that corner where you must crouch? Why choose a part of the room that forces you into a particular posture? What choice does that leave you with?

Some choose that they might easily choose again (so they believe). They choose anywhere spaces: four feet off-center and to the left of the center of the room, five feet two inches and to the southeast of the doorway. Their height minus their birthday, like choosing is math.

If they left the room without somehow marking their space (with tape, say, which is not allowed, which is cheating), they would not be able to find their precise part of the room again. I say "their" precise part, but it isn't theirs—they wouldn't remember it. They say, Hey now, yes they would. They know their flat plane of floor like I know my corner. I call their bluff. I say impossible. The light has changed.

A flat floor is nowhere, yet I would know my corner anywhere. I chose it and I recognize it, over and over, as I recognize the skin stretching over the balled knees of my crouch, their ache.

Some say their choices are less visible than mine but still are choices. I say their choices let them forget they are choosing at all.

FIRST PERSON NO LONGER

Your mother lifts a teaspoon from the sink, the air a damp dishrag thrown over her shoulder.

You've left her with your breakfast bowl, your body no longer a golden thing flung backward on the lawn.

Around her, the four walls of your sadness repeat without season. On the stoop, your gloom transforms into an unsuitable haircut.

It's Tuesday under low maples. The birds call; one has been in an accident.

Old friends fragrance the air but are easily caught in updrafts. Your mother's door has been repainted. Home is not home yet.

You can no longer tell where your arm comes to rest in the dark. You can no longer relate the plotlines of situation comedies to close friends.

Now the door opens, and they are not your mother. They suggest a board game after dinner. Charades. You bludgeon your face against the hardwood floor, but no one guesses your meaning.

For the familiar mistreatments of your old life, you grow nostalgic. You recover people only to misplace them again. When you bend to stroke the belly of a bird on the sidewalk, its claw tightens around your finger.

That night, after dinner, the millions are whispering. You wonder which of them would feed you intravenously. You listen for the sounds that mean you and lay them inside your mouth.

SINGLE STORY

For months, Jan and Dan spruced and patched the holes in their marriages. On occasion, Dan would suggest that Jan take out a second marriage on Jerry. Just to free up some extra love while they waited for the next Mrs. Jerry to come along, Dan said. It was too bad the spousing market was so lousy.

Dan hadn't known what he was getting into with his first spouse, Vicky, who'd grown drab over the years. He hadn't factored in the upkeep she'd require.

Jan had been more cautious, choosing to marry small. But now she could accommodate Jerry no longer. His single story was tedious. She had invested too much in him already.

Vicky was on the market—for sale by owner, of course—and Dan said he was contemplating a price reduction. But Jan couldn't shake the feeling that Dan wasn't showing Vicky in her best light. He'd turned down several solid offers. And where would he be without Vicky's endless honey-do lists?

One morning, after Jan left for work, Vicky called Jerry. She was on to them, and she had no intention of losing Dan to a postmodernist hussy. The conversation left Jerry feeling small. This was not unusual. Jan routinely made him feel small, his efficiency no longer a selling point.

But now the smallness conjured a new uncluttered feeling. Jerry dialed the number Vicky had given him and asked for a meeting that afternoon.

The broker had lots of tips. Jerry could knock down a wall, to appear more open, for example. "It's not your size that matters," the broker counseled, "it's what you do with it. And in this economy, a small marriage is just about all anyone can handle."

When Jan got home that evening, Jerry had already taken himself down to the studs. It turned out Jerry had solid hardwood under their years of shag and linoleum.

Jan began to question the kind of home she would make with Dan—what was the term, Neo-eclectic? Was that even livable space?

Three months later, Vicky remained unsold and Jerry was transformed. The bedroom was still not his best feature, but the new gas fireplace that hung like a silver egg in the corner of their living room suffused Jan's hearth with an animal heat. She ran her eyes over Jerry's gleaming floors, up his walls to his perfectly flat ceiling. Why hadn't they tossed the popcorn years ago?

A wave of exhilaration rolled through her.

"Jerry," she gushed, "let's do something to celebrate. Let's take out a second marriage. What do you—"

There was the sound of a key in the lock. The front door swung open and in stepped a young woman, contract in hand. "Oh, *this* is perfect," she said, entering the kitchen and running her hands over Jerry's granite.

"Jerry?" Jan stammered, her foundation suddenly shaky. "I don't understand. Are you with me?"

Jerry smiled gently and took her hand.

"I'm sold, Jan," he said. "I'm totally sold."

BAKERS

Some made loaves. With these loaves, some fed multitudes. Rumors spread about their origin and content. The loaves left everyone satisfied, and every year more appeared.

Some made rolls, easily consumed in a sitting. Delicious with fillings, accompaniments, but no meal in themselves. The rolls came three, six, nine to a bag. No one bought a single roll; no one recalled the best roll of their lives.

Some made crumbs. They hid their loaves and rolls away until they staled and could be smashed with a hammer under cover of darkness, or underfoot inside a sturdy bag. They were sprinkled from great heights for the birds or absorbed unremarked into other recipes. Some say these crumbs, under the right magnification, resembled loaves and rolls that stretched into a miniature infinity.

But the real crumbs were crumbs only, had never been anything but crumbs. They began as what they were, imperceptible to anyone but their makers, who, when questioned, would speak only of sensing their way, as if stepping continually into a moving spotlight in an otherwise stone-dark indistinctness. There was only the stepping, stepping, as if following a pre-laid trail to who knows where. Theirs was the true bread, already unmade, elemental, impossible, but nonetheless bread.

RISEN

The day begins with the eggs well hidden. Colorful eggs, magnificent painted eggs. They shiver in the dewy grass, in the low breeze. They murmur to each other, *Mother, Mother. Find us.*

He traipses across the lawn in a large, pink rabbit suit, replacing the eggs with candy. The children don't want candy. They want good real eggs to save from the chill of morning and set under an incubating light. They want life, not sugar.

The bunny suit murmurs, *here children, here children*, then takes up the eggs' murmuring, *Mother, Mother*. The eggs are confused. Is he one of us?

Through cloud cover, the sun blasts its drama of shadows on the lawn. The shaded grass turns ashen and the eggs are easy to find. Traipse, traipse, goes the pink rabbit, his basket overflowing with good real eggs.

But here, the rabbit drops dead as a moon. He has been hit by a meteorite! He has been hit by Love's arrow! The children swarm him and the good real eggs wail, *Mother, Mother*. Each child gathers an egg and cups it, holds it to their ear. The eggs fall silent, believing themselves safe, and the children run off in the many directions of their adulthoods.

NARRATIVE

Nobody considered me and I survived, so now nobody considers me and I survive.

Nobody understood me and I survived, so now nobody understands me and I survive.

Nobody put me first and I survived, so now nobody puts me first and I survive.

Nobody bothered to confirm that I was cleaning my teeth adequately and I survived (with cavities), so now I don't clean my teeth adequately and I survive.

Nobody let me know what the plan was and I survived, so now nobody lets me know what the plan is and I survive.

If somebody considers me, I won't survive.

If somebody understands me, I won't survive.

If somebody puts me first, I won't survive.

If I bother to clean my teeth adequately, I won't survive.

If somebody lets me know what the plan is, I won't survive.

ORIGIN STORY

In the beginning, they were Red, Yellow, and Blue. They didn't call themselves *primary* because they were *only*, and there was no context for comparison. Despite being three, neither did they compare themselves to each other. Rather they took turns ruling their creation, and each of their rules lasted a thousand human years. Red was blood, iron, and fire. Magma bonded the plates of continents. The humans spewed and fumed and forgot, their rage fired to nothing in the kiln of prehistory. Yellow was pox, pollen, and ire. A dull spell that drew sharp lines between peoples. The sun melted all the snow. Blue was water, sky. No land. The humans swam, if they could, or they drowned. Red, Yellow, and Blue were despondent. Each had managed to kill their creation. *We are too unsubtle*, they said. *We are too much ourselves. Let us mix that in our mixing we might create something new.* From their efforts came the age of Green, then of Purple, of Orange. Lush, and pure, and bright! The humans thrived, emerging from each sleep to a fresh, if makeshift, magnificence. Still, the labor of their mixing, of their being not quite themselves, took its toll on Red, Yellow, and Blue. Their novel beauties clamored to be fundamental again. And this is why beauty vibrates, why peace picks at the scabs of war.

THE RED PAINTER

Today the artist paints in red. He wants to paint in red. He is the red painter.

Today the artist wants to paint in red. Yesterday he painted in red. It is good that he paints in red. He is the red painter.

Today the artist wants to paint in blue. But he is the red painter. The artist paints in red.

The artist again wants to paint in blue. Blue is the wrong color. People will not recognize him as the maker of blue paintings. He is the maker of red paintings. He paints in red.

Today the idea of painting in red makes the artist swell with rage. All this time he has been wasting his time with red and red paintings. He should have been painting in blue. He has wasted so much time. He does not paint.

The artist wants to paint in yellow. If he paints in yellow his days as a painter in red will be over and his days as a painter in blue will never begin. Yellow is an entirely new project. There is neither the time nor the mental space to be a painter of red, blue, and yellow. Even if he were to try, people would say to him, "what happened?"

He paints in yellow, then he paints in green, then he paints in purple. It is absurd. None of these colors are him. He paints again in red. He is bored. He should have been painting in blue all along. He has wasted so much time with red but to abandon red now would be to invite censure. What is wrong with red, they will say. You are the red painter, they will say. What is wrong with you, they will say.

He paints in blue. He experiences ecstasy. He wishes never to stop painting. He has trouble returning to his regular life, to his wife and his children. His home is filled with his red paintings and the red paintings of others. No one has made a blue painting before. He is despondent. How is it possible for him to continue, with painting in blue consuming his every thought. He does not sleep.

He paints in blue. It is nothing like painting in blue yesterday. It was all an illusion. He has fooled himself again. He tries to paint in red but finds he cannot.

For several days, there is no painting. There was no painting. There will be no painting.

The artist sits. The artist feels tender toward his old works. He sees that they are good, that red is him after all. But he does not know if he can go on painting in red. This is farewell.

Today the artist takes the day off. He goes biking in the mountains. He goes sailing on the lake. He eats oysters and makes love with his wife. He knows she likes his red painting. This is farewell.

Today the artist paints in blue. He wants to paint in blue and he does paint in blue. He is the blue painter. He gets a call from someone asking him to be in a group show with two of his red paintings. They do not want his blue paintings. Please, the red paintings, they say. He says he will think about it.

Today he thinks about it. He sees that he is the red painter who is painting in blue. The blue paintings are the same as the red paintings; they only look completely different. The person who wishes to exhibit his red paintings is too stupid to see this. Otherwise they would take his blue paintings. They are the latest paintings. They are the real paintings. Only the artist can see this, the project behind the project, the foundational questions to which every painting—in red, in blue, in yellow, in green, in purple—is the answer.

REAL AND TRUE

My first wife was my fist. I pummeled my wife into life and made way for myself. When she was spent, I took my foot as my second wife.

With her I ran hard and far and achieved great distances from my beginning. I ate fine foods and my mouth watered, so I took my mouth as my third wife and we lived together for years in our bounty.

But she grew sour and bored, so I took my eyes as my fourth wife because the eyes cannot see the mouth no matter their contortions.

But the eyes, prone to slumber, were unavailable half the time, so I took my heart as my fifth wife out of need for a steady presence. I felt I could not live without her so large was my true love for my fifth wife.

But her steadiness cast my fickle nature in a poor light and I felt I needed a truer match, so I took my lungs as my sixth wife, because, like me, they cast out whatever they took in. But I did not wish to be cast out, so as my seventh wife I took my blood.

This wife I soon found too internal, too terrifyingly inaccessible, so as my eighth I took my skin, which was satisfyingly always ready at hand.

On occasion this wife broke, and my seventh wife leaked out and threatened me for a time, staining everything I touched. Then, all of my other former wives colluded to unsettle me—my mouth to spill her contents onto my feet, which would not move me aside; my eyes squeezed tight against any spirit of helpfulness; my first wife wanting to smash herself into everything, threatening to break my current wife further still.

But my eighth wife was unflinching and soon recovered and made me whole again. When inevitably I thought of taking another wife, she seemed to be in evidence everywhere I looked. And so, unable to escape her, I was made real in true love.

HOW WE CHANGED

After the baby came, the farm was gone. We didn't sell; it fell away. The sheep foundered; the pigs ate their brothers. For a long while, nature said nothing.

When I moved my head to the left to the rhythm of the music I heard, my vision blurred. The dogs' tongues lolled summer long. We endured a small impartial catastrophe.

In the end, the baby held up the world, which accommodated by adjusting its weight. Sleep hung like frayed strips of cotton in the trees. One by one, the night flung them down.

We lay our hearts over our eyes, arranged them vertically between our thighs, a place that required new versions of protection, no longer innocent or ours or fully intact.

Dear world, may we live with our memory of this sweet time lifelong. May his small world-holding body remain as he grows out of our arms into life's and others' arms. May the farm return, slow but persistent, the shy leaves unfurling their nutrition, ready to be eaten deep into winter.

This is the wisdom of what is granted: vegetables, bees, a Friday under sunshine, brighter than any holiday. We stored the pigs in the smoke shack and made what, from a distance, resembled snowmen with their fat. We use everything now. This is our only rule.

STARRY NIGHT

Take 138: Meryl Streep and Christopher Walken have lost their child in a storm. The townspeople gather with them on the gray beach. The sand is heavy, and Meryl realizes that her child is buried beneath it. She is screaming his name into the sand. The director yells "Cut," but Meryl does not stop screaming. "No mother would," screams Meryl. "Mothers scream forever." The buried child is not the child of an onscreen love affair with Christopher Walken but, Meryl tells herself, her own child who cannot breathe inside the wet sand. Meryl screams for the director to end the day's filming so she can resume her digging and screaming, unscripted. The woman Meryl plays in the movie believes her child is dead and is not supposed to dig. She is supposed to throw herself on the sand. But Meryl screams and will not stop until she has unearthed her child, until she has dug "all the way to China," as her costar Christopher Walken likes to put it. Now the director resumes the scene and Christopher Walken joins Meryl on the sand. They both scream and dig, and the director, seizing upon the shape of their agony, edits out the sound. His audience will marvel at the twisted mouths of Meryl and Christopher, and beyond them, the massive wave. The audience will see in the wave the slick, black heads of a thousand seals. They advance and smother Meryl and Christopher, and the movie is over. The baby is crying. It is 2:30 a.m. I go to him in the dark. He is moaning and crawling blind in his crib, bumping his forehead on the bars. He hears me and quiets. I lift him out and the milk comes strong, spilling from his mouth onto his cheeks and chin. He gags for a moment and then drinks deeply.

MOTHER AND DOUBTER

On a bench, two women. One smokes a cigarette while the other sniffs a sprig of lilac. The smoker is younger than the sniffer. The sniffer's stomach somersaults.

"Won't you put that out?"

"You know I can't."

"I know you won't."

"It's an addiction. I can't help myself."

"You might start with trying."

"I've tried trying. Sniff your lilac. I'm almost done."

The smoker takes a long drag and flicks the butt to the pavement. It lands a few feet from the sniffer's white sneakers.

"That's a fire hazard. Stomp it out."

"You stomp it out."

"You're impossible."

"You don't even *know* what's possible."

"I'll show you." The sniffer lays her lilac on the smoking butt. The smoke curls up in plumes between the purple clusters. Steaming grapes, thinks the sniffer. A steaming pile of—

"Flower trumps fire. Nice."

"You've got the spring and summer ahead of you to make firm your resolve."

"I don't want to get fat like you."

"We're out for a walk, aren't we?"

"I don't see you walking."

The sniffer sniffs and looks across the water. Impossible. The smoke curls at her feet. She rehearses the poem about fog and little cat feet, looks, and then urges herself, move on.

"I know why you do it."

"Don't flatter yourself."

"I do."

"I doubt it."

"It's a metaphor."

"I doubt it."

"For feeling smokin' hot."

"Ha," laughs the smoker. "I doubt that."

The sniffer rises, stretches her arms over her head and then swings them limply around her body. They are, she thinks, like fat whips.

"Hey, watch it. You almost whapped me in the head."

"I doubt it."

"You did."

"Doubt it."

"Did."

"Mo-ther."

"Daugh-uh-ter."

The smoker rises and bumps the sniffer's hip with her hip and they both move on just as the next moment arrives.

ONE POSSIBLE DISCOURSE ON GOD

The god of the heart only has eyes for the lungs, which house a god in love with the discourse of bone.

The ribcage is threaded through with a god who adores adipose tissue, which is riddled with gods who spend all day admiring the lean femur, the phalanges' agile links.

Meanwhile, the gods of the fingers honor the wrist, which itself worships oxygen—free as any thing a god can imagine, namely, anything but a god. The omnipotent skin loves the hair and the hair loves the mouth as it opens.

The god of the mouth wishes to be the god of tongues, but the tongue identifies spiritually with the teeth, all grind and rot.

Which gods care for us best? Gods who peer out of other bodies, wishing to occupy ours, or our gods who plot continually their own escape?

Dear gods, we love you.

God of eyelashes and pubic hair, god of saliva in love with bile, god of myelin in fear of electrical impulses and any matter that moves faster than the admirable methodical bowel.

May the god of arms reunite in spirit with the shoulders, who, we pray, will learn to forgive the god of the neck. O nose, O earlobes of holiness! We know you by the names we call you. We monitor your place in the sentient dark.

ISABELLE AND THE TRINITY

The humans were at their mortality again. Isabelle lay bedbound, listening, praying, listening for answers. The Son's body, crusted and scabbed, tended by the angels of lichen and moss, lay always underfoot, a beat dog, each mortal blow a new blister. Through each death—though not Isabelle's, not Isabelle yet—the Son grieved for the Ghost, who ached for the Father, who, having wandered into some new wilderness, pined for no one, finding his old creation a ponderous bedmate. Lying concussed in her childhood bed, Isabelle dreamed of the Trinity, of the Ghost that lay between human and divine, Father and Son, of the daughter homespun, handmade, hidden somewhere at the periphery of philosophy. She had fallen from her horse, a dappled gray. She was not to sleep, a doctor's order, her mother planted at her bedside, making sure. But her mother had died three years before. The weight of her mother was a ponderous bedmate. The Trinity was a mystery and could not be solved, unlike her mother, who could not be solved but was no mystery—rather, a plague of tragedy that tightened itself round Isabelle like a wood louse that would not unfurl. Isabelle had survived their accident, had, despite her natural inclination toward obedience, not been wearing her seat belt that day. Hurled through the windshield, she had sustained a shattering but no death. Her mother, belted, had died sure enough. How the Ghost moaned and wished to be Isabelle, O girl, O impenetrable one. The Father farted in his new kingdom, magnanimous in his nonplus, and the Son, shaken by the sudden sound, surrendered more flesh to the firmament.

ABOUT FACE

The sole problem with Bill's relationship, as far as Bill could see, was that every night, when he clapped off their bedside lamp, casting them into darkness, Janice's face migrated to the back of her head and gestured extravagantly.

This wouldn't have been so bad were it not for the frantic sound her eyebrows made against the pillowcase and the simple knowledge that when he draped his arm across the small of her back, her soft breasts yielding to the firm mattress beneath, her eyes were almost certainly staring up, unquiet, at the ceiling fan.

Janice had informed him of her peculiarity early on, and, initially to her delight, he had tried to catch her face in the act. No such luck. When he clapped on the light, or, in his stealthier attempts, whipped the flashlight from beneath the covers and blasted it at her head, her face was back where it had always been, on the front, the mouth smiling broadly. The only way to confirm the event was through blind touch, when, in darkness, he encountered first hair and then, later and toward the back, the ridgeline of her nose, which had always made him think of New Hampshire.

Was this a true problem, Bill agonized, or only the sort of thing that seemed like a problem but wasn't? True, as Janice pointed out, parts of Bill's body, too, routinely changed shape in the presence of certain stimuli. At least her face didn't engorge or excrete.

And wasn't it *his* sensitivity to light, *his* inability to sleep with even the faintest glow, that began it all?

Wouldn't they be rid of the problem altogether, Janice had persisted, were it not for his tenebrous appetites?

It was the potential, Bill bellowed into the blackness, *the potential* that when he needed her face, it might not be there!

Where? Janice's voice floated toward him.

Where he needed it to be! His finger stabbed at the darkness above her neck.

But his words sounded hollow even to him.

NOBODY'S HOME

I've bought a small plot of land. I want quiet and to escape my neighbors at the condominium. The plot is filled with divots and pocks that belong to a vast anthill. No matter. I have ant poison back at the condo.

In the morning, I shake my poison into the ground. I have signed the papers and scrawled the check for the earnest money. Now I will build my own small house. I unload a pallet of bricks and spend my evening back at the condo soothed by my favorite television characters.

The next morning, back at the plot, I find my bricks have vanished.

"Vandals," I mutter, burying a pang of doubt about the neighborhood. I have another pallet delivered and cover it with a blue plastic tarp, for protection.

In the morning, the bricks are gone again. The blue tarp lies off to the side like a crinkled lake. The divots in the anthill have been disturbed, but I can find nothing else suspicious.

I decide to spend the night at the plot in my tent. No television, no neighbors. I listen for the wind, but all is still.

At dawn, the ants take me underground, where they have been building my brick home. They have blocked out "Nobody's Home" in a pattern of bricks along one side, not quite understanding. Still, I'm touched. Who has cared for me like this? The ants give me a tour of my house, and it is as I had dreamed it. They've stocked the fridge with my favorite foods. A large television hangs in the living room.

The ants insist I spend the night. They feed me and ask gentle questions about my childhood. I have too many beers and share everything—my loneliness, that evening in the dark with my mother—and they listen, their shining eyes moist and reflective. I tuck myself into the bed the ants have made for me and am soon asleep.

In the morning, the coffee pot has brewed six cups. I pass from room to room, sipping at my mug. There isn't much natural light. I hadn't noticed that. I gulp coffee to quash a pang of anger at the ants and burn my throat.

I spend the day watching my favorite characters. I feel not myself. My abdomen is distended, and nothing in the fridge is appetizing.

But the ants have thought of everything. A rumbling overhead produces gashes of noonday sun. I peer up through the new skylight in my dining room at the ants waving down from the condominium they have built on my plot. I remind myself it will be nice to have neighbors; the muffled activity of others can be such a salve. The ants have reproduced the sentiment in cross-stitch above my toilet.

But my neighbors have thumping techno parties and do not invite me. They binge drink and throw their empties onto my roof. I call up to them, "Please, I'm trying to sleep, I want only to sleep," but no one hears me.

BART AND ELIZABETH

The midcentury modern lamp that Bart bought to arc like a moon over his living room has come with a lizard after all. This despite Bart's recollection that he did not check the box next to "lizard, the ultimate accessory for the midcentury man." The lizard, contrary to the description in the catalogue, is not content to languish on the lamp's marble base, needless as an air plant. Neither is the lizard modern. It is primitive and makes no effort to ingratiate itself.

Bart calls the company. It is Thursday, noon, and he is home on another sick day, in case the woman he met two weeks ago calls. He does not want to miss her call, but he has call waiting and surely will hear if another call comes through while he is discussing the matter of how to return the lizard.

Bart dials. The lizard licks its eye. A woman's voice answers and Bart relates the problem.

"She's a gecko," replies the woman.

"Is a gecko not a type of lizard?" Bart says. "Anyway, that's beside the point."

"You will need to keep her warm," the woman says.

"I don't want to keep the lizard at all," Bart says.

"Gecko," the woman says. "She'll be laying her eggs soon."

The lizard darts onto Bart's Nelson bench and vomits something yellow.

"Sulfurous beast!" Bart yowls.

"She has morning sickness," the woman says. "You might be more sensitive."

Bart moves to inspect the damage. The lizard raises an amber eye and shoots a long pulpy tongue into the neatly trimmed stubble on Bart's chin. The tongue sticks there briefly before retracting.

"Ughh."

"She kissed you, didn't she," the woman says. "I bet she just kissed you."

"She's disgusting."

"That's what you all say at first. Just give it a few days and then see how you're feeling."

The lizard has scampered up Bart's trouser leg and is clinging to his button-down, which billows like a sail with her weight. With a fleetness seldom associated with the heavily pregnant, she springs from Bart's chest to the top of the bookshelf. The impact of her departure leaves Bart winded. He gasps for air. The woman on the telephone informs him that the company will not refund him the gecko surcharge unless he agrees to keep the gecko. Light-headed, Bart agrees.

That night, Bart wakes four times to the lizard's cool body, pressed first to his armpit and later, repeatedly, his groin. A closed door cannot stop her. A locked door with balled socks wedged between it and the floor also cannot stop her.

By Friday afternoon, the lizard's calisthenics have stripped the glamour from Bart's lamp. He calls in sick again, intent on preserving his domain against the lizard's foul habits, and has started to reimagine the lamp as a weapon that might be pitched over opportunely. Bart cannot bring himself to kill the creature directly. The death would have to be oblique, almost unintended.

In the morning, Bart finds six leathery eggs under his bedsheets. His leap off of his Tempur-Pedic scatters the eggs, and the gecko—Bart is not given to speaking in the generic once enlightened—springs into action and with deft moves gathers each orb into the impression Bart's body left in the memory foam. Bart notes that his impression is slowly lifting, the mattress expelling it, as if he were a foul odor.

Bart calls the company again.

"This is a good sign," the same woman says. "She's settling in. You're keeping her warm. Doesn't that make you feel good?"

Bart glances at the gecko, her cool body around the eggs.

"She's not like the old generation that laid their children and left them to fend for themselves," the woman continues. "She's modern."

"What's your name?" Bart asks.

"Elizabeth, but please, call me Liz."

"Liz," says Bart.

***

Elizabeth hangs up the call. She enters Bart's first and last name at the bottom of a long list of lonely men. Another happy customer. While she waits to field the next complaint, the company manager appears at her desk.

"Congratulations, Elizabeth, you've reached your quota," he says, loud enough for the others to hear. "Again."

He takes her hand and shakes it, forcing her to rise from her chair. The headset slips from the back of her neck.

"Pack your bags—your tropical beach vacation awaits you."

Elizabeth opens her mouth, her tongue springy.

"No need to thank me, young lady. You know the routine. You've made many a lonely man far less lonely and given many a modern lizard the stable home she needs to raise a real family. Good work. You're a real firecracker."

Elizabeth nods. She knows. She is their top-selling agent. She pulls her suitcase from under her desk, and the manager hands her another one, empty, with tiny holes punched along the side.

"Now go and get us some more good girls," he says, patting Elizabeth on her slim rear. It cools at the touch.

THE WIDOWER

Jim noticed his wife had vaporized about a year into their marriage.

"I haven't," she said, her head wagging on the end of her neck.

There was no telling her otherwise. Jim began to second-guess himself and tried to resume their usual habits. But it seemed that a wind whistled through his wife's throat. He missed the fragrant bloom of her voice.

"Claudia," he said, "my cloud princess."

"Come off it," Claudia puffed.

Gently, sadly, Jim obliged and came off of Claudia. He withdrew his extendable ladder from her cumulous bulk and lowered it to the lawn. On his way down, he noted the gutters needed emptying. He'd stayed away too long.

"Farewell, my gossamer love," he called to her. "Until we meet again."

"Off with you," fumed Claudia.

That night, Jim was restless. The pendulous shape of Claudia filled their bedroom with night shadows. Occasionally, a small piece of her wafted in through the open window and settled next to him on their bed. It seemed to want something from him, but pressure of any sort, even his breathing, forced it into retreat. It attempted to hide from him by shifting shapes on the pillow: a fluffy kitten, an oven mitt, a snake. How wonderful was his Claudia! How he ached to possess her again! Jim drew closer to the frantically morphing piece of his wife and, in their marital darkness, inhaled deeply.

DUMPSTER

Fluids, her husband liked to remind her, could be either a liquid or a gas. He spent his days in a university lab pouring fluids from one test tube to another. She spent her days in their faculty apartment imagining him in the act of pouring. To end the imagining, she'd chew three peanuts, in quick succession, until they formed a butter in her mouth.

Fluids conjured bodily fluids, also part of her imagination, though she'd like nothing better than to never think of their bodily fluids in states of relation. Once, she told him she no longer wished to be his wife, that she found him repellant.

To this he had replied, "I, too, at times, find myself tedious."

His reply did some work toward increasing his appeal for her—he was a fellow human, after all, it seemed—but it burned off like butter left in the pan.

Their apartment was in the west wing of a large, brick dormitory. Every afternoon at two o'clock the garbage trucks arrived in the parking lot below their bedroom window. All the dumpsters campus-wide were arrayed there, and the garbage truck made its way down the line, lifting each and tipping until its heavy lid clanged open as prelude to the act of emptying. She had imagined that she, too, might become a giant receptacle, but the months cycled by and nothing grew.

She came to anticipate the daily emptying. It was for the good of the community, whose productivity would be unsustainable were it not for this counteracting emphasis on emptiness. She imagined again her husband at his pouring. She considered the tiny puffs of gas that might escape with each pour, that if he poured a gas back and forth long enough, he would find himself with nothing. Was it the same with liquids? Perhaps with liquids the emptying would take longer. She imagined pouring a viscous liquid—vaginal fluid came to her mind, which was surely not a gas—back and forth infinitely, or until it had been poured entirely away. She chewed three peanuts, then another three. From her window, she watched the truck's mechanized arms welcome the necessary refuse of others.

Once, as she watched the driver complete his task, he had waved at her. She had stepped back from the window and retreated to their bed, where she slept for hours, waking only to the sound of his key in the lock.

LUCK

I find, in a single day, six four-leaf clovers. My luck will change. I wait, but nothing does change. Nothing perceptible anyway. Perhaps something imperceptible has changed. I listen for it. But my family does not increase, in number or in wealth. My stable job does not transform into a better stable job. My husband does not bring me flowers any more frequently, and the ones he brings are no more glorious than usual.

In the belly of the earth, the beast fingers its list, abdicating catastrophe after catastrophe.

NO STUFF

When she threw away the children—a decision that, at the time, had followed quite logically from her mass purging of their beloved objects—she suspected she had gone too far. But by then the house was gone, demolished for its excess of dust, its irrepressible beetle life, its tacky residue, left by her children's stickers on the walls around their beds. All that remained was her marriage, but that was the curse of the chronic declutterer: to have married a man so lacking in self-regard that her acerbity—a foil for her monumental need to be empty—fell upon him as a warm, fragrant rain. There had been that time he'd called her an asshole on Facebook, but that had only, if briefly, stoked the embers of her love, because then he too became again a thing she had once wanted and now could throw away.

THE INVISIBLE PROPERTIES OF THE HUMAN

The first is the scent of apples fermenting in the throat. The second is the vast territorial amnesia of the years before five, with which the scent of apples is associated. The third is the apple, still on the tree, the flower not yet the apple, the bud, the seed, the nitrogen fixing itself in the soil. The fourth is the nostalgia of potential, sending me backward and forward simultaneously to arm buds sprouting on the torso, to arms crossed on the chest in death. The fifth is the first, that scent repeating. The sixth is the suspicion that comprehensive self-knowledge is impossible, that the only self to know is the self today, the self here among us, writing, reading what is written, revising what is read. The seventh is magical because seven is a magical number and must not be understood. The eighth is the impulse to pleasure oneself in the moments before sleep, an impulse associated with the vast territorial amnesia of the second invisible property of the human, which, in this case, is the inability to know whether my father was fundamentally a real or an imaginary friend.

NEITHER HERE NOR THERE

I am not from here, but I no longer live where I am from. Where I am from is far away and here is near, but I am not from here. If I stay here for many years, will I one year be from here? No, I am far from where I am from and the years of being here only make there farther
away.

ALL THE LITTLE DEATHS

When we arrived, the first row of little deaths was already lined up shoulder to shoulder along the firing range. It was easier to pick them off that way. The rest extended in single file like rows of blighted corn. The little deaths in the first row shivered but held firm. Douglas had trained them well. We were to use BB guns—it was the only way Douglas could guarantee their cooperation. Nothing too violent, they'd requested. Resilience wasn't in their nature, the littlest deaths being easily bruised, and skittish. We had to warn them when we were going to fire by raising our hand in a sort of salute. That was the arrangement, elaborated in the weekly emails Douglas had dispatched in the months before the big event.

None of us had unreasonable expectations. No one expected any big deaths to show up; no one expected to take out their own big death. This was simply about making life easier on a day-to-day level. Some of us sought to extend the shelf life of certain foods. If the little deaths that caused them to sour or stale could be stalled—via BB, for instance—the food would last longer, which would save us money, freeing us to spend it on more pleasurable pursuits. Others were more ambitious. They didn't want to avoid death per se, but rather sought to win a protective advantage for certain body parts. One woman had a nasty canker sore that blistered, wept, and crusted over. She wanted the little death to leave her upper lip alone, long enough at least for someone to fall in love with the rest of her.

I stood in line and watched as, one by one, my brethren took the BB gun in hand and picked off their row. We'd all been practicing our shot. The little deaths were flying backward, a purplish mist trailing after them as they landed, stunned, in the grass or staggered about, clutching their arm or stomach. I felt almost sorry for them, except I knew how much they had taken from me.

Just then a hush fell over us. Trish had set aim, skipping the salute. Douglas leaned in, then seemed to think better of it and took a step back. Trish held herself still, staring down the gun at her little deaths, who fidgeted and avoided eye contact, but held their ground. What was she up to? Then, with a practiced swiftness, she lowered the gun, wrapped her lips around two fingers, and whistled. Tweet! All of Trish's little deaths and all the trim rows behind them poured in one mass toward us. I heard Douglas scream "No!" as Trish wheeled around and began firing. I was hit first in the arm and then again in either thigh. Into each small, nonfatal wound leapt a little death. I fell to my knees. I thought I heard the singing they say you hear when your big death comes to collect you. But it was Trish.

Trish was singing to us, "My friends! I love you! I am setting you free! Your big deaths will never get you now!"

Then she turned the gun on herself, and in a hail of BB fire, the little deaths roared into her.

THE WAXING OF MARNI

Her children's ears were eternally dirty. No matter how hard and often she cleaned them, the infernal dirt returned. To Marni, the dirt was diabolical.

Up close, the sulfurous beads collected as if hastened by time-lapse video.

"You're hurting," Marni's children cried when Marni dug at the wax.

Marni was not a dirty person. She was a tired person, an ambivalent person, a passive aggressor. The wax, Marni knew, made her a bad mother.

That night, their father put the children to bed.

"Clean their ears," Marni called, steadying herself against the mattress. Sleep was pressuring. She climbed into bed in her underwear.

"Insert the Q-tip gently," said the dream.

By morning, the wax had billowed from her children's ears into the hallway, sealing their bedroom door. Their father was not in bed; Marni intuited that he had succumbed already. But in the muffled house, Marni sensed the steady rise and fall of her children's chests.

Marni pulled on her silk chemise and dove into the wax. God and Satan were there already.

"Dirty, dirty, dirty girl," they said, with practiced collusion. They smiled, high-fived.

Marni clawed at the slick walls, but the cavities caved with more wax. Marni stretched her mouth wide and gnawed her way through, the goo hardening in her teeth like a yellow lava.

"Chew, chew, chew, you dirty girl," Marni muttered.

God and Satan took their cue and began to chew their ways out, too. It was a blessed solution.

With the head and the heart honchos gone, Marni felt the wax soften. She rounded the corner to her children's room and could discern their forms beneath the layers, their gentle undulations.

"Mama's coming, Mama's here," Marni gobbled. And she tunneled toward her offspring, teeth yellow, like a vole.

IMMORTALITY

In a windowless room, a child plays jacks before a blue rectangle of light and water. The child hasn't named the fish that swim inside the water because she knows that in time names become obvious. But the fish stay small, their details out of reach of her peering eyes that see only the singularity of things. The fish breed and there are more fish and more, and the pace of their lust overwhelms the child. Each day, she must scoop the dead, their bodies wafting among the living like untethered kites. She tosses and scoops her jacks, drifts in and out of consciousness, and wakes each time to a new catastrophe.

The child proceeds to divide her fish. She sets like to swim with like in new blue rectangles, the bright fish with the bright fish, the gray fish with the gray, the fish who swim with a bent spine with the other bent fish. In the original tank are the original fish, glutted on delectables and commanded still by the child to grow large rather than many. But the fish do not obey, do not know even that the child is there beyond the incandescent blue, the gentle sucking action that, on occasion, carries all their waste away. The room grows crowded with watery cubes, rectangles, and cylinders that glow in the child's darkness and themselves grow crowded, the fry and eggs imperceptible amid the crash of scales. One day, the child places her jacks in a row and begins to name the fish: Earth and Heaven, Neutron and Mountain, Mother and Father. And the naming is never over, is without end.

ARITHMETIC

Ten people write ten songs and give them to ten other people.

One little person writes one big song, and one big person smashes it to smithereens and gives them to twenty thousand people.

Ten people take the ten biggest songs and lock them in a vault until the little people have paid.

One big person writes a little song that one thousand people enter and, dreaming, cannot escape.

One person asleep in one big song dreams that the big song makes her so small she is visible only under the magnifying glass of dreaming.

The people take their smithereens and over generations piece the song back together, singing it to their children and their children's children. The words do not fit together anymore and instead make thousands of new songs, some big, some little.

Ten people bury the ten littlest songs in the ground, pressing an ear to the dirt only when it is safe.

One big person throws one little person high into the air, singing all the while, and the little person grows wings and lives forever, but only after falling hard to the ground where one song ends.

BALLOON

The others deflated in due time, their affectionately drawn Sharpie faces shrinking with the loss of air. But Blue Man remains, his taut features expressing the same winsome exuberance with which five-year-old Ben had drawn them now years ago. Neither has Blue Man's latex yielded to the powdery whiteness that spelled disaster for Yellow Man, the only other in Blue Man's litter to outlast the others. Yellow Man's tie-off, like Blue Man's, had seemed truly air tight, and his expression of wide-eyed wonder had endured from Ben's birthday in mid-December to almost the following Thanksgiving. But Yellow Man was not Blue Man, and there could be no shame in that. Not one bit. Ben had kept Yellow Man's crumpled form in his treasure drawer for three years, until exigency trumped affection and Yellow Man entered the trash. Alone, peerless, Blue Man roams the floor of Ben's bedroom noiselessly, his sheen as brilliant as the day Ben released into him lungfuls of his boyhood. It is this memory, Blue Man decides, that allows him to persist. Ben's cheeks aching with the effort, and Blue Man made real, in that ache, like the other beloved objects. He carries Ben's breath from one corner of the room to the other, aided at times by the weather through an opened window, or, in winter, by forced air. He is too large to be lodged under Ben's bed, so he roams in full view, too bright for hiding. In all those years, no one has popped him. Blue Man senses now that the humans in the home, even Ben, fear him. He smiles at this thought, as he smiles at every kind of thought he has. He drifts and smiles, the contents of Ben's long-ago exhale into him a thing everyone agrees is best kept contained.

LAST WORDS

Be cautious when approaching the scholars. Their slim daggers, while not fatal, make wounds that reopen every year, like a community swimming pool.

Be cautious, too, when approaching the scholars' spouses. They are oblique to the field of action but never tangential. They know the angle at which the dagger must be thrust, and they manufacture the blades.

Beware the children of the scholars and their spouses. They have borne the worst of it and know the arguments that cannot be won. They have stored their unused last words in secret cupboards and will use their words, sharpened over years, to end you.

Behold those ended by the words of the scholars' children. Their faith is a shield of air. You'd think their faith would permit them to circumvent a fatal argument, but thinking is what got you there, not faith.

And what is faith? Be cautious.

WHAT COULD HAPPEN TO ANYBODY

No matter how angry Anybody became, no matter how calm, Nobody could die. The possibility of Nobody's death pressed. In the heat of argument, here again were the paramedics bursting in, hauling Nobody off to hospital. Anybody, in their right mind, pondered the origin of the arrangement; had it always been so? Anybody could try to shrink their anger, make it small, maybe enough to hurt Nobody but certainly not to kill. Shrinking would hurt Anybody, too, while on the outside things grew large, like Nobody dying, over and over. It would seem to Anybody, then, that nothing and everything was happening, but always to Nobody. These things couldn't happen to Anybody. One day, Nobody asked Anybody, *What do you feel?* Nobody had died again, that constant negation, that constant absence. Anybody could have suffered it. Anybody, but not Nobody. *What do I feel?* Anybody repeated. It was Anybody's guess.

MOVIE OF THE DAY

TAKE I

Quarter to midnight, you drop me at the hospital for my night shift. I walk, a wall of glass between us, and forget to wave as you pull away, missing your fatal crash with the ambulance. I work for hours not knowing until I get the call. I leave early and you're home, hunched bloody over a cup of coffee. Your hands are blue. "What happened?" I beg. I'm falling to my knees. "It was only a movie," you say, "an action scene."

TAKE II

That afternoon, we scale a small local mountain. The dappled ground shifts beneath us as we scramble to the top. There, the broad and shining lake, the wheeling birds, crying out. You look suddenly sad. "I wish I could fly," you say. "I wish I were a bird." And you step toward the edge, your face a knot that slips and drops away. I scream down the trail and find you sprawled on your back in the grass. "Join me," you say. "It's a picnic. It's something I threw together to surprise you."

TAKE III

Driving home, sated on rotisserie chicken, we chat about the day's events. I'm happy, but my arm shoots out and grabs the wheel. The car squeals into a telephone pole and bursts into flames. You're screaming. Your seatbelt is jammed. The car blazes around us. You grab my arm, your hand a cinder on my skin. You cry, "I never meant to hurt you. It was all a joke—the crash, the jump—but this, why did you do it?" I try to answer, but my lips catch on my teeth.

FISHMONGER

In the domain of the dead, my father apprentices to the fishmonger, private counselor to recent suicides.

There, it's all about self-preservation, which my father models by packing the newly dead in rows on ice in that giant display case in the sky. Now, if only a good fish would come along and take his dead home as companions for their winsome fry.

He's also in charge of the towels, which he tears into handy strips and dispenses with welcome-to-the-area kits packed with broken glass, lengths of rope, a polished loaded gun. The dead can do themselves in as often as they want. *You get good at it*, my father soothes, *and slowly, the urge to self-murder recedes.*

My father has such humor now. He's got all his dead in stitches. When he tucks them into their beds of ice, he jokes with them about the fish. How in life we were to master the trick of sticking together, to relish life near the surface, where the warm spots gather.

But never mind, my father assures them. *The fish children are delightful. You can't lose. Not here. Not ever again.*

THE SON GOD

The day God intervened, Harry was in his backyard, deciding whether to go to Bobby Nichols' house or return to his mother in the kitchen. The sound of her whisk against the metal bowl declared meatloaf, which declared Thursday, which was just like any other day. Harry didn't want to play with Bobby, a boy to whom the most amazing things happened just before Harry arrived.

The day, for example, that Bobby had found, finally, the other sock.

"Guess what," Bobby had said.

"What?" Harry had answered, obediently.

"Aw man, you just missed it. I was going through my drawers, looking for my money, you know, and there it was, out of nowhere. Aw man, these are my favorite socks."

Bobby had shoved the sock at Harry, insisting upon a closer inspection.

"You should've seen my face when I saw the sock, I bet I looked real funny. Aw man, I'm so happy. And it just happened, just before you got here!"

Bobby was always happy, Harry had to give him that. Harry wondered whether his pleasure at thinking about the mystery that death implied about everyone he knew had the potential to make him as happy. He thought he felt a smile on the inside sometimes, but he couldn't be sure what his face was doing.

It would be dinnertime soon. He could feel his mother at his back through the kitchen window, stirring the meat. Harry bounced his left hand a little, testing its weight. In it was Bobby and suffering through another of Bobby's stories. In his right hand was his mother, massaging eggs into the meat. If he chose her, she would ask him in to help. He liked helping her. He had a nice mother. Maybe she was staring at the back of his head that very moment, wondering what he was doing there, just standing, his hands cupped slightly at the end of his arms. Overhead flickered the black-green leaves of late summer. He would go to her, help her like a good son.

The impact sent Harry flying backward several feet, and he landed hard on the metal bulkhead under the kitchen window. First, there was thinking, then flying, then his mother scooping him up. He saw the underneath of the door jams as they passed from the yard into the kitchen and the living room, where his mother, who only moments before Harry had cupped in his right hand and chosen (again and again he had chosen her), laid him on the couch. Her mouth was moving, but her words burned in the blaze of yellow light that filled their living room, its edges expanding and receding in a sparkling dust. God was huffing and puffing in Harry's house. Should he have chosen Bobby? Was that it? Was it always wrong to choose your mother as the heavier of two known objects?

The detectives searched the yard as dusk fell. Finally, one entered the house carrying a strange rock in his hand. He said he had pried it out of the bulkhead. The bulkhead would need replacing, unfortunately. The rock had practically busted it in two.

"I think it's a piece of a meteor," he said. "Kid, it could've taken your hand off."

"The hand I was holding my mother with?" Harry asked.

The officer looked at him.

"You might take him down to the hospital, Ma'am. Make sure every-thing's all right up top."

The policeman tapped the side of his head.

"Concussion."

The purple sky of early evening sat beyond the black leaves. Harry didn't get to keep the rock. After those moments in the living room, he never saw the rock again, never saw the hard knot of God that like a fist had sent him flying. Harry looked, but God didn't stay, never did. At the hospital, the doctor painted iodine onto the scrape on Harry's left hand and became the second adult that day to tell him he was lucky the rock hadn't blown his hand right off. Harry pictured his arm with nothing at the end of it. No mother, only air.

Back at home, Harry's mother settled him on the couch with pillows and a blanket and put on the video she liked to play whenever he "lost his cool." The images glowed before them, the infant and his mother's breast hefted toward his gaping mouth.

"See how happy you were," she said. "You can always be that way, if you choose it, Har."

His mother waved at them from inside the TV, cradling the baby and smiling. And she sat next to him on the couch, her feet tucked up under her, watching with him in the blue light, until it embarrassed him less to look than to turn away.

IN SEQUENCE

before. the beginning. where jobs were available. return to the center after the marriage goes bad. at the end of it a birdwatcher weighs the good against the grammar. also at the end of it a telephone call a play written for television. this was not a bad job after all. he was skin and moans. all man christ all truth beyond all doubt all bets were off. but only for a standard amount of troubles. crime spent by the seaside. he leapt beautifully. he landed on all fours. knee and hand action on a make-believe desert. he landed himself in jail spelled the new way and with wire. this was not a bad joke after all. he tried the american three-way conversation where opportunities were put to a boy he used to be. but the boy couldn't see beyond the grave. there were circumstances beyond him entirely and an italian wine pressed. his gray matter was very serious. a decision in a time and in a crisis. there he sat himself entwined inside and rainy. after. the end.

BARRY AND THE BOULDER

The boulder on Barry's back keels like a mighty Viking ship, forcing Barry to throw his weight this way and that, quite haphazardly, if only to remain standing.

At first, Barry had courted the boulder, finding his back too straight and uninteresting. He had thought that lodging it there might help him to attract women. He dressed to accentuate its size. But more often, it seemed, it got in the way, especially in the bedroom. Some women seemed more interested in its content—the kind of rock it was exactly, the geologic pressures responsible for its shape and appearance—than in Barry, who found himself in these moments wedged between the women's nattering and the boulder's primeval hissing and popping in sympathetic, if unintelligible, response. Barry would be forced to raise his voice, which inevitably cast him as the killjoy of the group, and the women, scowling as they struggled to zip themselves back into their dresses, left.

But tonight, Barry's raising his voice does not do the trick and he feels forced, in his state of being heartily unheard, to raise his fist. And to raise his fist, he must first throw back his shoulders and stand straighter than ever and, quite by accident, as a sort of side effect, Barry puffs out his chest for the first time in his life. At this moment, the small portion of the universe Barry is occupying—meaning Barry and this woman Brenda and the few cubic feet of carpet that hold their bodies and the distance between them—falls silent, and the boulder, quite gracefully for something of its heft, rolls off Barry's back. Brenda is stunned and rushes to it to make sure it has not been injured. Finding it intact, she scowls at Barry as she struggles to zip herself back into her dress and leaves.

Now Barry is alone, face-to-face with the boulder. It is nothing like he remembered. It is quite a bit smaller. Not tiny by any measure but more the size of a bucket than a pirate ship. Neither has it the sharp-edged, granitelike appearance he had recalled. Rather, it is covered in a soft green moss through which tiny purple flowers peek. The side of the boulder that had pressed against Barry's back is matted down and has a bruised aspect, as if it needs tending. Barry tries gently to fluff the moss on this side, and the boulder winces and then falls into a fit of wild sobbing on Barry's lap.

FUTURIST METHODOLOGY

In anticipation of a first conflict, a woman creates an equal-and-opposite second conflict to offset the first. In anticipation of the second conflict, the woman creates a third conflict, which pleases her until she realizes it is identical to the first conflict. This, the woman realizes, is the source of her conflict, and she labors to create another to offset it. The woman is tired, but there is no way to offset fatigue without sleep, and sleep will mean leaving her existing conflicts un-offset. The woman offsets her desire for sleep with a desire for resolution. In the meantime, her bed begins its nighttime routine without her.

ONCE YOU START

On his way to the bathroom in the near dark, Dave stubbed Dave's toe on the door jam.

"How could you?" Dave roared. Dave's toe had always been so insensitive.

To retaliate, Dave slammed Dave's foot into the bathroom cabinet. That ought to do it. Dave's toe was silent, but Dave's foot yelped inadvertently.

"Oh, man up!" Dave raged, and Dave whacked the back of Dave's hand against the wall, a minor punishment for Dave's hand's sympathetic throbbing.

The alarm sounded in Dave's bedroom. Dave raced to turn it off and tripped, slamming Dave's knee into the wooden chest at the foot of Dave's bed.

"Unngh!" Dave's mouth said, uninvested in the outcome, having only to admit food and shape the sounds that came from Dave's body.

Dave's eyes released a fiery liquid.

"Don't you start," Dave warned Dave's eyes and preemptively flung Dave himself backward into the living room. But Dave's plush rug intervened. Dave scrambled to his feet and hurled Dave's upper body headlong into Dave's bookshelf, which pitched forward in collusion. Finally, a lousy co-conspirator! But Dave's body rolled out of the way, and it was all Dave could do to keep Dave's right arm outstretched long enough for Dave's bookcase to sear it against the hardwood floor. Dave wrenched Dave's arm from under the bookcase, its laminated edge tearing into the moist fiefdom of Dave's underarm.

"Take that," Dave said. Dave's arm lay quiet. Dave's shoulder began its whimpering, but Dave had heard it all before.

PUCKER UP

Liselle has a small bump just below her clavicle. She rubs it, stares at it, raises her arms over her head to see if it makes her skin pucker. It doesn't.

Now Liselle's husband mentions a lump on his neck. Liselle inspects her husband's lump, says it looks more like a bump, and tells him about her bump. Go to the doctor, he says.

Liselle does not go to the doctor. It is a bump, not a lump. She rubs it, turns sideways to discern its profile in the mirror, raises her arms over her head, looks for puckering. The bump is sore from the rubbing and is red.

"Why are you so red?" ask the bump's supportive tissue.

"I don't know," says the bump. "She keeps rubbing me."

"She thinks you are a lump," concludes the supportive tissue. "Play it cool."

The supportive tissue was always saying useless things like "play it cool." Temperature was a function of health. Health was a function of function. The bump could not play it cool if it wanted to. It lived close to the breast, close to the heart. The bump wished the supportive tissue would shut up.

The bump began to like the idea of being a lump, but it played the fantasy close to its chest.

At night, when Liselle's Body was prostrate, the bump swelled as far as its edges would go. Not very.

"Chill out," said the supportive tissue.

The bump began to feel alien in its own Liselle's Body.

Liselle continued to poke at it.

"Quit it," said the bump, uncomfortable being shoved up against the supportive tissue, which began to recede in irritation.

Were it a lump, the bump reasoned, they would cast it out. Then it would be free to pursue its own life, its own interests.

The bump dreamed. And between dreams, it boiled with fantasies about excision and being tossed into a stainless steel bowl or made dizzy in a hyperbaric chamber.

One day in the shower the bump said to Liselle, who did not, could not, listen, "I fear something has come between us." Disconnected, the lump drifted into Liselle's left armpit, where the supportive tissue was particularly sensitive.

"Shut up! Shut up!" screamed the tissue, seemingly without provocation.

Liselle raised her left arm, stared and poked. Then she puckered her lips and kissed the bump goodbye.

SUMMER AT THE LAKESHORE

Dennis sat on a patch of grass near the bike path to prove that life was arbitrary and brutal. Two of Dennis's species glided by on bicycles, decimating vast cooperative assemblies of ants. Dennis watched as the ants hoisted the crumpled bodies of their kin underground. The cyclists laughed; one of them was funny.

Dennis clamped his eyes shut, craned his neck to the left, and opened them. Bright dandelions in leagues of grass.

Now the cyclists stared at the lake. In the air, millions of iridescent gnats. The cyclists swatted, smiling, at the air, sending mother gnats into ruinous collision with father, sister, and brother gnats. Their filigreed bodies littered the ground.

Were Dennis, with one giant hand, to yank the cyclists from their bicycles and stomp their faces into the pristine gravel of midsummer, his actions would almost certainly be misinterpreted.

Around him, acres of ungrateful lawn. Now the cyclists had ice creams and were consuming billions of enterprising microbes—a flip attempt at summer gaiety. Dennis could see—Dennis's hands slid out and away from Dennis's body—how the small waves lapped and lapped. His fingers laced themselves into the dumb green blades and pulled and pulled and pulled them from the ground.

TREATISE ON HAPPINESS AND SADNESS
FOR THE REST OF US

We begin with simple statements:
The rest of us are happy in spite of ourselves.
The rest of us are happy to spite ourselves.
The self is a dark and sooty bird that makes a nest of happenstance and calls it happiness.

*

This is a mistake, but only for the philosophers, who take everything literally. The rest of us are heading for the middle of the lake in small bleached sailboats.
We throw ourselves from one side to the other to keep our boat from tipping over.

This is known to the rest of us as staying afloat.

*

The rest of us, in other words, may be in the same boat.

*

Meanwhile, the philosophers hoon ahead on jet skis to study the bigger picture, namely, that the lake is bigger than we are in our keeling boats, deeper and wilder.

The philosophers have tremendous accidents and turn entirely apoplectic over certain turns of events as they try to avoid brushes with the rest of us and our precarious middling would-be happiness.

*

The philosophers want to know are the rest of us poets (*yes! yes!*) of great sadness or of great hope in spite of great sadness.

We tell the philosophers we are poets of great sadness in spite of great hope, but this makes the philosophers crazy.

*

Now that we have the philosophers' attention, we capsize our boats and hide beneath them with our store of air. The philosophers deduce they've lost us forever and call our names in Greek, Latin, French, and German, but we don't respond. As usual, we don't understand.

*

We are happy beneath our boats being sad and lost.

We imagine how we must look from shore, like so many tiny sun-bleached islands, ancient islands, each with a god beneath.

*

Seagulls land. Their feet shift like stars in our dark dome—*such happiness!*—and below us, another greater expanse of darkness, and some of us, seeing the fish dart in the weed like silver eyes, grow afraid.

*

Some of us turn our boats back over and lie in their bellies, pretending death—*what a hoot!*—pretending the lake has consumed us.

*

But we fail to impress. Our philosophers have taken to talking to nature of nature, forgetting us again—our chapped lips, our parched throats setting their theories to action like a good rabble, which is to say, we believe that a human paid no attention will not survive.

PLOT

Once, I stood in childhood, and not wishing to remain, I fled to the grown-up countries. Only then did I think to keep one print of a buckled shoe where I began, near the phantoms my parents became.

It used to be I could purchase my own square foot in childhood, a place to return to and stand on, my own solid ground. The arrangement was ancient, grandfathered in. But for me, among the newest adults, still vividly sensing my childishness, there is no foothold available. My ancestors have retained their plots, never intending to return. No one valued childhood then. They'd simply placed a check mark in a box next to a number in a square on a map, as if selecting a seat on a long flight. Life looped. The plot that once stood favorably in a bright meadow now sits under pavement outside a stranger's door. Meanwhile, I have difficulty recalling earlier times, the lessons of my joys, the heralding scents of my disappointments. What had been the pattern on the quilt on the bed? What had been the bed?

Because all is forgotten, all does not register as loss. All the happy days and all the sad, patches of green receding. When some alien sensation rises in the body, it unsettles rather than clarifies.

Shall I clamor for the ocean to be plugged with soil, so that no less than the dead must relinquish their plot to the living? Shall I need that ground to bear me forward, as a parent urges a child to school, calling from the swept threshold, "I'm here. I'll see you later"?

ALL YE FAITHFUL

We assemble because assembling produces the feeling of assembling. We bring our family, because families give assembling that family feeling. The scent of a child's washed head, the pliant fat of a cheek: these are experiences that produce experience. We wear navy because navy is respectable. We wear a hand-me-down tie because to feel connected to another is to feel connected. We like what we like because what we like is attainable, and it's best to feel satisfied at least some of the time. Must we go on dreaming, dreaming, with no dream to be a dream come true? Late at night, our lamps off, we rehearse the logical implication of His faithfulness, which without the possibility of faithlessness is an empty prospect. We permit ourselves to discuss the potential for His infidelity, feeling ourselves through that talk rerooted in wonderment, just as we had planned when we first planned to be serious believers.

IMPLANT

IV

knowing how something is going to end and watching anyway is different from watching something you have already watched before *like when you throw bodies into water and they start swimming* you get used to the movie and when the movie is gone it takes a while to get used to the silence *you might think of a baby in a mother sitting lakeside* every child in America went straight from third to fifth grade *fourth grade may or may not exist* it is a lie invented by the government an implanted memory

IV

knowing how something is going to end is different from watching the government *like throwing movies into water and watching them swim* you might think how quickly things unravel *inside her life coiled tighter still* a baby in a womb is an implanted memory *it takes a while to get used to*

IV

fourth grade went straight from third to fifth grade *every child in America is a body thrown into water* knowing how something is going to end is different from a baby *from getting used to the movie life coiled tightly* fourth grade is different from something *you have already watched before* knowing how something is going to end is getting used to every child in America *you might think of a lie invented by the government* the precedent doesn't exist

IV

the precedent is a lie invented by the government *you might think of a life thrown into water* you might think you could just start swimming *when the silence is gone it takes a while to get used to every child in America* it is different from watching the president get used to the baby swimming in the mother *when the movie is gone it takes a while* to sit lakeside *bodies in water are implanted memories* the water takes a while to get used to

BUBBLES

From below, the humans shout at us.

"Look how high! It's going to pop!"

We do our best to ignore them, but for the record, we do not "pop." We lose our boundaries.

Our light bodies compel, swirling, iridescent. Some of us couple, in twos and threes, even fours, but none of us remark on it. We are above comment.

Some of us have lived a full five minutes, our splendor impervious to the air. Others have drifted so high who can say if they aren't still drifting, looking down from their great vantage at the thin and vulnerable, the moist, newly blown.

Below and beside us sit the baser creatures—mailboxes, trees, telephone poles. We could do without our symbiotic relationship with the humans. Except, of course, the breath is essential, if only at the very beginning and only in combination with the foam from which we come.

MORTAR FROM MORTAL

Here are the people carrying their houses on their backs. Their houses are worthless, stripped, and flammable. Their backs are dark with tendons.

Faced with losing their houses, the people tend to imagine the two as inseparable. Here are their tendons grown up through the foundation: concrete block, stone, brick, woven of the same material, which in human terms is always flesh.

A pound of flesh for a pound of house. In a vacuum chamber, each pound would plummet at the same rate: house of feathers, house of lead. In an antigravity chamber, we would all be laughing at the daily news of falling houses and the tendencies of people to mistake them for asteroids.

Feathers and lead and antigravity.

In the beautiful neighborhoods, an ounce of prevention is worth a pound. The houses glow, yellow with firelight, yellow against blue snow.

Here are the people setting their houses on fire. Here are the people selling copper wire, aluminum siding, plastic fencing. Here: here are the people. Take them. Divide them as you see fit. Cut the mortar from the mortal. They are dead weight.

They don't know what to do with themselves.

SELF-SOWN

As a sign of their love and commitment, Joan gave Pete a self-sowing vagina to affix on his lower back, a discreet location but one that, under the right circumstances, would sufficiently announce her ownership. Kate gave Mitch one too, but on his forearm, which made dressing awkward for him, especially in summer. Still, Kate was worth the trouble. Susan placed hers on the underneath of Julie's right foot, counting on the extra stimulation it would impart in the course of Julie's daily activities. Each of these women, and many like them, relied on the slight but not inconsequential effect of the vaginas to ward off paramours. And it worked—until, that is, some men began giving self-sowing penises to their lovers. Some men were sensitive in their placement of the member, while others, true to their nature, placed them in untenable positions, on their partner's forehead, for instance. And just as love becomes its own unpredictable bloom, so too did the self-sown genitalia unfold their own appetites, in this case almost exclusively for the self-sown genitalia of others. So it was that another sexual revolution was born, complete with its own cohorts of winners and losers, thieves and knaves.

HOLE IN THE WALL

She woke and no longer had a mouth. Rather than shaping words with her tongue and lips, she simply thought them, and they entered the world through a small hole in her face.

People seemed not to notice what was missing. Some called the small hole a mouth, but she knew better. Her mouth was gone forever, if ever she'd had one, the way things are gone in dreams.

She might find it later impressed on the side of a building, telling secrets to a stranger. She would like to be that stranger. Still, she knew what her mouth would say: *Father, father, father, farther, farther, farther, farther.* It was the only secret it knew. She would recognize her mouth anywhere, but how would it know her? She would be no better than another building or another stranger.

Would the mouth, like the rest, be fooled and call the small hole in her face also by the word "mouth"? Who would call a hole a mouth, and equally who would mistake a mouth for a hole? There on the public wall, it nattered on, making something into nothing. She walked away, rehearsing a small tight song of loss.

A WOMAN OF NO OPINION

To avoid forming an opinion of either the rich or the poor, she resolved to think about neither.

When thoughts of either group pressed, she replaced them with a list of trees: Mountain Maple, Marlberry, Myrtle of the River, Hickory. But many were introduced species, sown to remind the wealthy of other places: Mimosa, Royal Paulownia, Tree-of-Heaven.

So she replaced her list of trees with a list of states of water, starting with the many names the Inuit have for snow: water white, water cold, water frosty. But these were merely different concepts, which she too had: blizzard, slush, slurry. She then had to admit to romanticizing the Inuit for her own gain—that is, to avoid thinking about the rich or the poor in order to avoid forming an opinion of either.

She indulged briefly in imagining faces sorrowful and red with cold. She wished to have no opinion about sorrowful faces. She wished to see them as not sorrowful, or rather as sorrowful and not sorrowful at the same time.

But she had read on the Internet the plight of the animals they lived among: the polar bear, the narwhal, the walrus. She could not help but think they would be sorrowful over their destruction, just as she, in spite of herself, is sorrowful when she apprehends her ornamental crabapple glittering with a green-gold helmet of Japanese beetles.

She wishes to have no opinion about the Japanese or their beetles.

The Japanese didn't introduce the Japanese beetle to her garden; that was the work of the sly tycoon who first brought the iris to America. It was on a shipment of iris bulbs from Japan sometime before 1912 that Japanese beetles crossed the ocean to these shores.

But she wishes to have no opinion about tycoons. And the iris, after all, is such an elegant flower, and Japanese beetles do not feed on irises.

How the colors of the iris accumulated! The deep purple of the wild variety, its yellow throat, was everywhere and made her think of the poor. The glistening pink falls of a bearded specimen hovered before a champagne flute. The rich, it seemed, were also everywhere inside her.

She stared hard at her walls, bare, as she wished to have no opinion about color that might sway her mood one way or the other, which in turn might sway her in the direction of the rich or the poor. Her inner alarms blared.

WISDOM STORY

I find the braid in a drawer in a hotel in a big city, I find it in a hole in a forest. I think *murder*, the hair a body part left over. I shove it in a Ziploc bag, carry it with me through life. It is a rare find, talismanic in the darkness it may or may not point to. When I need to feel tentative, I lift it from the bag and hide it in my house. I hunt for it, and on finding it, I experience its horror, its lure, as if for the first time. Although the braid unfurls in places, from overhandling, its capacity to suggest is not diminished. Perhaps it has grown. The braid is older. So am I. We both know more.

SMALL POTATOES

Pete was in the kitchen singing "The Battle Hymn of the Republic" again. From her camp on the couch, Marjorie feigned the dead man's float. Pete was a pacifist, but he liked a good call to arms.

"What do you want for dinner?" he sang. *Glory, glory . . .*

Potatoes float, Marjorie thought dimly, gathering her thoughts into a pile. *They bob.*

She hefted herself onto her back. The ceiling remained a popcorn ceiling. Marjorie calculated the potential effect that her rising from the couch might have on Pete's mood. Best not to introduce energy too suddenly. "What do we have?" she called. She'd keep it neutral.

Pete poked his head and shoulders through the low pass-through, his eyebrows almost to his hairline with excitement. "A smorgasbord of delicacies! Dehydrated, canned, and frozen!"

There is never enough, Marjorie reminded herself, rising slowly to her elbows. Best to avoid a head spin.

"We have Mexican, Asian, Italian—you pick! Take us, my damsel, on a culinary tour of the pantry!"

The loud thud that earlier had emanated from the small closet they'd repurposed to hold their cans and boxes stalked into Marjorie's mind. "You've packed it too full," she said.

Pete looked at Marjorie. Lamplight had always heightened her beauty. He could see through the windows that the sky shone cool with late day, the trees an occult blue-black. He recalled the suitcase he would pack each year for his family's lake vacations, his mother sitting on its lid, laughing as he struggled to close it over every necessary item.

"What was that thing you made that one time, with eggs and beef? It had black beans in it, right?" Pete rooted through the stacked cans. "Here," he said, producing a can of black beans, "we have them!"

Marjorie looked. The unwashed pot on the counter behind Pete made him appear old, tarnished. Perhaps by her.

"You refused to eat it."

"That doesn't sound like me."

"Well, you refused, and then you ate it anyway."

"That's more like it."

"Because I cried, because I told you it reminded me of meals from my childhood."

"Aww, Marjorie, let's not talk about that again. It only makes you sad."

"You mean it makes only *me* sad, or it makes me sad *only*."

"It makes me sad, too, Marjorie, to see *you* sad."

Pete hovered, but at a respectable distance, thankfully now a smidge less buoyant. The pantry door was closed. Now, she could think. She gathered the bobbing spuds. Such a friendly word: spuds. It boded well that she had used it.

"How about couscous? We could put raisins and pine nuts in it and serve it over lettuce with a side of edamame."

"We don't have lettuce, at least I don't think—"

"Did you look?"

"Let me look. Oh, we *do* have lettuce." He was getting excited again. But it was nervous excitement. Marjorie could deal with that.

She did her best to sound dour. "I thought so. So, does that work? Couscous with raisins and pine nuts over lettuce and edamame?"

"Are we going to mix the edamame in with the salad?"

"I thought this was my tour," Marjorie said, surprising herself by managing to face Pete. One of her eyes winked.

Pete smiled his boy's smile. Marjorie's mood was lightening, but she didn't need Pete getting giddy again. She didn't need another sad night. "You go ahead," she said. He returned to the kitchen. The pass-through framed his T-shirt moving across his stomach as he gathered ingredients.

Sitting upright on the couch, she closed her eyes. There was the seesaw, always at the ready to balance and weigh. She saw Pete on one end and a Pete-size sack of potatoes on the other. Perhaps the sack of potatoes was just slightly larger than Pete. Perhaps she was the sack of potatoes. No, she was in the middle, as herself, the human Marjorie, one leg on the beam balancing Pete and the other on the beam balancing the potatoes. Her legs channeled her weight equally so that her feet were like blocks of metal welded to the beams holding Pete and the potatoes in midair. "Don't drop them," she counseled herself. "Just hold steady."

She felt heavy on the couch, heavy with the effort of holding steady, and her separate parts seemed to roll slowly away from her. Then, Pete was there—*Glory, Glory, Hallelujah*—hovering over her, reaching into her, carrying parts of her into the kitchen. He held her heart over the sink and started peeling.

PLACEHOLDERS

We didn't get the house, but the insistent monument of the Second World War urged us onward. They didn't have our brand of cornflakes, but the Loch Ness Monster nevertheless coaxed gentle souls toward Scotland. We didn't get a raise that year, but banners flapped over Japan, the tattered flags burned to a white dust. We didn't venture out, though the waves beckoned to us, bearing the great barnacles shoreward. We didn't overcook the rice, but still the volcano indulged its temper and the orangutan nursed its third child. We didn't get the tickets, but the weeds grew tall and the leggy flowers taller, carousing with the winds of late October. We didn't conceive a child that year, but stars magnetized the air, turning the molten compost of the earth. We didn't go Christmas shopping, we didn't unpack the boxes, but the esteem one person can have for another bloomed again and again between us and our boy outgrew four pairs of shoes. We didn't cut any coupons, though the tender core of human need conceived some good new music. We didn't turn the clocks back, but trillions of 1s and 0s burned, chanting along their wires their obsession with us, *yes, yes, no, no, yes, yes, yes.*

ACKNOWELDGMENTS

I wish to thank the publications where the following pieces first appeared, in some cases as verse:

1110: "The Invisible Properties of the Human"
Barrow Street: "Mortar from Mortal"
Bartleby Snopes: "All the Little Deaths"
Chimera Review: "In Sequence"
Columbia: A Journal of Literature and Art: "Implant"
elimae: "Treatise on Happiness and Sadness for the Rest of Us"
Harvard Review: "Death Devours More than Nadine"
New England Review: "Real and True," "Mountain," "The Red Painter"
Pleiades: "The Jar," "One Possible Discourse on God"

Green mountains of gratitude to my Vermont writing group: Alison Prine, Karin Gottshall, Kerrin McCadden, Major Jackson, Didi Jackson, Ben Aleshire, Maria Hummel, Eve Alexandra, Jari Chevalier, Emilie Stigliani, Rachel Daley, Bill Stratton, Meg Reynolds, Kristin Fogdall, Holly Painter, Elizabeth Powell, Tanya Lee Stone.

Beyond Vermont, endless thanks to Craig Morgan Teicher and Brenda Shaughnessy, for urging me to gather what I had into a book, and always to Mary Cappello and Jean Walton, necessary sparks and paradigm shifters.

Abounding appreciation goes to Jenny Molberg, Bridget Lowe, and everyone at Pleiades Press for transforming a manuscript into a book. Thank you to Kazim Ali, for opening the door, and to Bill McDowell, for allowing me to feature *Untitled (ice on grass)*, from the Almost Canada photography series, on this book's cover. I am grateful, too, to the Vermont Studio Center, where some of these works were written.

For combined decades of encouragement, I thank Miriam Kienle, Nomi Hague, Joelle Jensen, Maeve Eberhardt, Annie Murray-Close, Joyce Cellars, Anthony Grudin, my sisters, Catherine Karapuda and Mollie Grace, and my mother, Robin Grace, who modeled the creative life by being unable ever to stop painting.

Long love poems go to Steve Budington, who paints in all the colors, and to Finn and Vita, who are still choosing theirs.

ABOUT THE AUTHOR

Penelope Cray was born in Australia and was naturalized as a US citizen on September 11, 2018. Her poems and short fiction have appeared in journals such as *Harvard Review*, *New England Review*, *Bartleby Snopes*, *elimae*, *Pleaides*, and *American Letters & Commentary* and in the anthology *Please Do Not Remove* (2014). She holds an MFA from The New School and has been a fellow at the Vermont Studio Center. She lives with her family in northern Vermont, where she runs an editorial business.

THE ROBERT C. JONES PRIZE FOR SHORT PROSE

Robert C. Jones was a professor of English at the University of Central Missouri and an editor at Mid-American Press who supported and encouraged countless young writers throughout a lifetime of editing and teaching. His legacy continues to inspire all of us who live, write, and support the arts in mid-America.

The editors at Pleiades Press select 10-15 finalists from among those manuscripts submitted each year. A judge of national renown selects one winner for publication.

ALSO AVAILABLE FROM PLEIADES PRESS

The Imaginary Age by Leanna Petronella
dark // thing by Ashley M. Jones
Destruction of the Lover by Luis Panini, translated by Lawrence Schimel
How to Tell If You Are Human: Diagram Poems by Jessy Randall
Fluid States by Heidi Czerwiec
Bridled by Amy Meng
30 Questions People Don't Ask: The Selected Poems of Inga Gaile, translated by
 Ieva Lešinka
The Darkness Call: Essays by Gary Fincke
A Lesser Love by E.J. Koh
In Between: Poetry Comics by Mita Mahato
Among Other Things: Essays by Robert Long Foreman
Novena by Jacques J. Rancourt
Book of No Ledge: Visual Poems by Nance Van Winckel
Landscape with Headless Mama by Jennifer Givhan
Random Exorcisms by Adrian C. Louis
Poetry Comics from the Book of Hours by Bianca Stone
The Belle Mar by Katie Bickham
Sylph by Abigail Cloud
The Glacier's Wake by Katy Didden
Paradise, Indiana by Bruce Snider
What's this, Bombardier? By Ryan Flaherty
Pacific Shooter by Susan Parr
It was a terrible cloud at twilight by Alessandra Lynch